Dear Professor Whale

MEGUMI IWASA

Illustrations by Jun Takabatake

GECKO PRESS

Dear Reader

What makes you feel happy?

    Is it getting something you've always wanted?

    Winning a race?

    Or being the best in a test?

    How about when you can eat as many treats as you want?

Do you remember Professor Whale who lives at Whale Point? Well, something has made him so happy, he's bursting to tell you all about it. What could it be? Shall we visit Whale Point and find out?

Contents

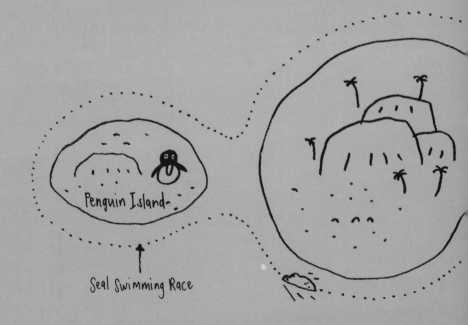

Penguin Island.

Seal Swimming Race

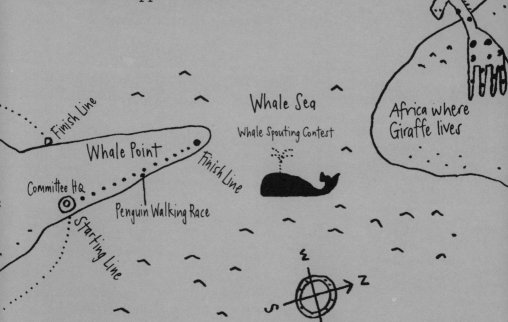

Professor Whale Loves Blue

Professor Whale gave a great big yawn.

"Now, now, that won't do," he told himself.
"I mustn't waste this fine day by dozing off."

Whenever he looked up at the blue sky or out
at the blue sea, it made him happy to be alive.
Blue was the thing he loved most in the whole
world.

Today, the ocean was a dazzling ultramarine.
Letting his old body drift in the bright blue
water, he gazed up into the clear blue sky. In
the distance, he could see something flying
through the air.

"I wonder what it's like to fly through the big blue sky. Just once, I'd love to try it."

He started imagining what he would look like, flying through the sky.

"I would need wings," he thought to himself. Enormous wings to match his enormous body.

And they would be blue, too, of course!

As he pictured himself flying gracefully on blue wings through the blue sky, he started to nod off again.

"Whoops! That was a close call. This is no time for napping!"

Suddenly he noticed that whatever was flying in the sky was coming closer.

"Professor Whale!" it cried.

He squinted to see who it was.

It was Pelican, the famous, hardworking delivery bird. Pelican handled airmail deliveries while Seal handled sea mail deliveries. Recently, they had both received a Certificate of Appreciation for their excellent work.

"So it was you!" the Professor exclaimed.

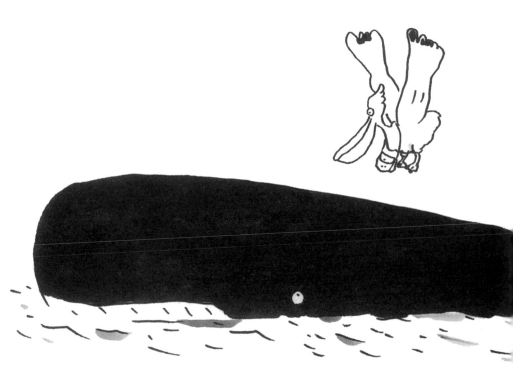

"Hello, Professor," said Pelican as he landed on the whale's enormous back. "Long time no see."

"Pelican, you really must stop calling me 'professor.' You know I've retired from teaching."

"That may be so, sir," Pelican said, "But you'll always be a professor to me."

"Still, I would really rather you called me... uhm...by a friendlier sort of name," the Professor said a little shyly.

"Really? Like what?"

"Well...ahem...just for example, you know...
Whaley, perhaps?"

Pelican cocked his head.

There was a reason why the Professor longed
to be called Whaley. Until quite recently, he had
been the teacher of Whale Point School. His
only student had been Penguin from Penguin
Island. One day, Penguin had received a letter.

What kind of letter?

A letter that said, "I am Giraffe. I live in Africa. I'm famous for my long neck. Please tell me all about yourself."

Penguin and Giraffe had become pen pals, and now they called each other Pengy and Raff. The Professor secretly thought it would be nice to have a friend who called him Whaley. It sounded refreshing, like the blue of the sea that he loved so much.

"Or if that doesn't work, how about Big Blue?" he suggested. "That's what everyone called me before I became a professor."

"Oh, really? Big Blue? Hmmm..." Pelican did not sound convinced. "Professor Whale, you're really very impressive and, well, distinguished, you know. Calling you Whaley or even Big Blue seems a little..."

Professor Whale was just wondering what "distinguished" meant when Pelican changed the subject.

"Oh, by the way—you've got mail."

He held out a letter addressed to Professor
Whale.

"Why thank you," the Professor said. "But
what happened to our delivery seal?"

"He had to deliver some letters a long way
away and won't be back for a while. He asked
me to fill in while he's gone," said Pelican,
puffing his chest out with pride.

"Poor Seal. Who on earth could have sent him so far away?" the Professor wondered.

"Well, I mean to say...wasn't it you, sir?"

Indeed, it was. Professor Whale had written a whole bunch of letters that went like this:

Dear You, Whoever You Are, Who
Lives on the other side of the Horizon,

I am Whale. I live at Whale Point.
My body is almost all head.
That's why I'm so smart, people say.

Please tell me all about yourself.

Yours sincerely,
   Whale at Whale Point

Pelican continued: "Seal told me since he'd already delivered your letters to everyone around here, he was going to try farther afield."

"Oh, that's right, that's right. I remember now." Professor Whale was a bit embarrassed.

"Anyway," said Pelican, "if you need any letters delivered in the meantime, please call on me." And with those words, he flew up into the blue sky.

Professor Whale opened the letter and began to read.

Dear Professor Whale,

How are you? I'm fine.

Quite a few students have started coming to my school.

But teaching is hard work.

Now I see how extraordinary you are, Professor. Because you're so good at teaching.

I'm going to do my best to become a terrific teacher like you.

I hope that you will stay my teacher for ever and ever.

yours sincerely,
Penguin at Penguin Island

The letter was from his student, Penguin. After graduating from Whale Point School, he had opened a school on Penguin Island. Now everyone called him Professor Penguin.

"Well, well. Penguin's working very hard by the sound of it. I suppose I can't expect him to call me Whaley either. But how I wish someone would..."

"Time for sleep, I suppose," he thought.

And with one huge yawn, he was asleep before he even knew it.

Seal Returns

Speedy, efficient, and hardworking: that was
the delivery seal all right! He'd told Pelican he
would be away for quite a while, but he was
back much faster than he'd thought. Although
he was a bit tired, he swam straight to Professor
Whale.

At that very moment, the Professor was
wondering why no one had replied to any of his
letters.

He gazed up at the sky, but there was no sign
of Pelican. Worse, it was a gloomy day, which
made him feel gloomy, too.

Just as he was thinking he might as well take
a nap, a familiar voice hailed him.

"Professor Whale! It's me, Seal. I'm back."

"Oho! Welcome home. Sorry to have sent you so far away."

Of course, the Professor was hoping that Seal had brought him some mail. But had he?

"I've got a letter for you, sir."

The Professor's heart lit up like a bright blue sky. "Really? That's wonderful!" He took the letter from Seal.

"I'll be off then. Let me know if you need me,"
said Seal, and he zoomed away.

The Professor's heart was pounding with
excitement. He had always wanted to get a
letter from someone he had never met, to feel
that special thrill.

"Who could it be from, I wonder? And where?"

In unsteady letters, someone had written "To Mr. Whale, Whale Point."

He turned it over. On the back it said, "Wally, Otto Island."

He had no idea where Otto Island was, and had never heard of Wally.

"This is exciting! Here goes!"

He took a deep breath and opened the letter.

Dear mr. Whale Who
Lives at Whale Point,

Hello. My name is Wally. I'm
a whale too. But I'm still
little. I live on Otto Island.
It's full of otters. I've heard
of Whale Point. My grandad
used to live there a long time
ago. But he got old and died.
Yours sincerely,
Wally at Otto Island

The Professor had been expecting a letter
from an animal he would never normally meet.
Maybe even one that was totally different from
him.

Otto Island was new to him, but this Wally
lad was a whale, just like he was.

Still, when he read that the young whale's
grandfather had once lived at Whale Point,
he was unable to contain his excitement.
He had to write back at once.

Dear Wally Who Lives at Otto Island,

Please tell me about your grandfather. I think I might have known him.

Yours sincerely,
 Whale at Whale Point

Wally's Grandfather

The Professor wrote "I might have known him" because it was also true that he might not. So many whales had once lived in the sea near Whale Point that the Professor could not possibly have known them all. The sea had been black with whales. That's why it was called Whale Sea and why the point of land jutting into it was called Whale Point.

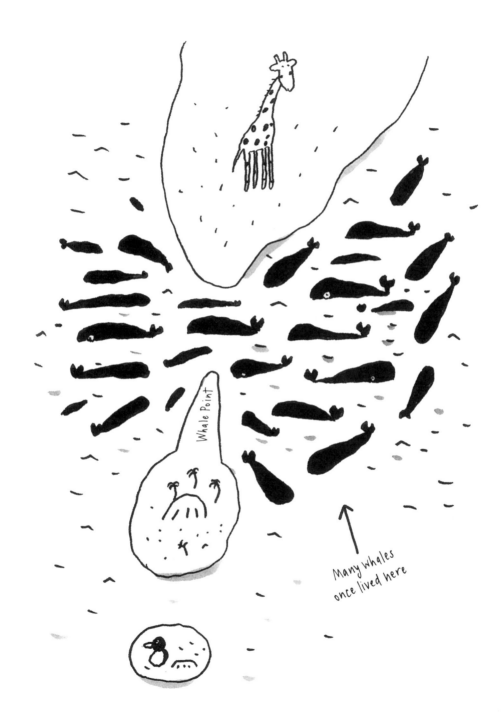

So why was old Professor Whale the only one left?

Well, there were once so many whales that eventually there was not enough for them to eat, and they had to move away to other places. The Professor's family decided to stay, but all the other families left. As time passed, first the Professor's grandmother and grandfather, then his mother and father, grew old and passed away. The Professor never married, and now he was the only one left.

As always, Professor Whale asked Seal to
deliver his letter. While he waited for a reply,
he thought fondly of the old days.

Soon, Seal returned with another letter from
Wally.

Dear Mr. Whale Who

Lives at Whale Point,

My grandad competed in the Whale

Point Olympics. But he only won

the silver medal. There was a great

big enormous whale that always won

the gold. How I wish I could

have seen the Whale Point Olympics.

Yours sincerely,

Wally at Otto Island

The Olympics were a regular event at Whale Point back when there were lots of whales living there. And it wasn't only for whales. Seals and penguins took part, too. The whales competed to see who had the strongest, most spectacular spout, and the winner was given a gold medal.

The Professor already knew who had always won the gold. That "great big enormous whale" was none other than himself.

"I see. So his grandad always won the silver," he thought. "That would have been Spout, surely? And that means Wally must be Spout's grandson..."

He remembered Spout very well. They had not only been rivals, but also the best of friends.

But now Spout was gone. Maybe all his old whale friends were gone and he was the only one left.

After all, he had lived for a very long time.

As the Professor's thoughts drifted, he heard
voices in the distance.

He listened. They were coming closer.

It sounded like someone was calling him.

"Ahoy there! Big Blue! Big Blue, ahoyyy!

Who could it be?

Whale Point Class Reunion

Huge black shapes raced towards him, surging through the waves.

They looked like whales. And not just any whales; they looked like some of his old friends. The Professor could hardly believe his eyes.

First came Bubbles, regular winner of the bronze medal. "Ahoyyy! Big Blue!" she called.

Next came Whistler, Bubbles' younger brother. "We got your letter!" he shouted.

A little behind him came another whale...

Who was it?

"Big Blue dear!"

Big Blue...dear?

The Professor was startled. Why, it was Bella Balena, his first love!

She must be an old lady by now, but still...

"What's going on?" the Professor asked. He was so happy, his voice squeaked.

"We read your letter and decided it was time for a reunion," Bubbles said.

"You're still enormous!" Whistler exclaimed.

"You haven't changed at all," Bella Balena said. "None of us have. Well, maybe we're all a little older."

Everyone laughed.

"So you're still alive!" the Professor said. "I'm so glad!"

Tears filled his eyes at the sight of these dear friends. When he thought about it, he had not seen another whale for a very long time.

There was only one friend missing.

"Remember Spout?" the Professor asked. And he told them what he had learned from young Wally.

The sun went down and night came, and still they kept on talking about the old days when they were young and full of life.

"Hey!" Bubbles said suddenly. "I just had a wonderful idea."

Everyone looked at her.

"Why don't we hold another Whale Point Olympics?"

"But we're too old for that now," said the Professor.

"Not for us," Bubbles said. "For the young ones."

Everyone's eyes shone.

"Count me in!" Bella Balena exclaimed.

"Me, too," Whistler said. "Let's start planning." He was raring to go.

There might be no gold medals for the Professor this time, but he suddenly felt full of energy again.

As soon as daylight came, he wrote to Wally.

OLYMPIC

Dear Wally Who Lives at ~~Otto~~ Island,

My friends and I have decided to hold the Whale Point Olympics again. We're planning it right now. We'd love you to come, too. I'll write again once we've decided on the details.

I'm looking forward to meeting you.

Yours sincerely,

The Winner of the Gold Medal Long Ago Who Is Now Just an Old Whale.

Getting Ready

The whales made lots of posters and put them
up all over Whale Point and places nearby.
They sent out lots of fliers, too.

WHALE POINT OLYMPICS

SEEKING CONTESTANTS FOR THE
FOLLOWING GAMES:

1. SWIMMING RACE: SEALS

2. WALKING RACE: PENGUINS

3. SPOUTING CONTEST: WHALES

PLEASE CONTACT THE WHALE POINT
OLYMPICS COMMITTEE
IF YOU WISH TO TAKE PART.

OLYMPIC

Whales, seals and penguins who were keen to compete began arriving at Whale Point. The Professor and his friends were in high spirits.

Wally set out from Otto Island guided by the delivery seal. This would be the first time he'd ever seen his grandfather's home waters.

A group of penguins arrived from Penguin Island with a big banner that said "Whale Point Olympics," made by the students of Penguin Island School.

Penguin's friend Giraffe had also been invited as a very special guest. He was already on his way from Africa.

Once again, Whale Sea was full of whales, although not quite as many as in the old days.

For most of them, this would be their first Whale Point Olympics, but they had heard lots of stories about it from older whales.

Day after day, the Professor and his friends worked late into the night organizing the events, the rules and the venues. It was a lot of work, but they hadn't had this much fun in years.

"Professor Whale, you've got a visitor!"

Seal swam into view. Behind him was a tiny little whale.

"Is that you, Wally?" the Professor asked.

"Y-y-yes." Little Wally was awestruck by the Professor's gigantic size.

"I'm so glad you could come. But what about your parents?" the Professor asked gently.

"I c-c-came by myself." Wally was very nervous.

"Well done, little one," Bella Balena said.
"You must be tired."

"We knew your grandad very well, you know.
We were all friends," said Bubbles.

Wally's face lit up.

"That's right," Whistler said with a grin.
"We were best buddies."

The enormous old whales told little Wally all about his grandad.

He may never have won the gold medal, they told him, but he was strong and brave. And that wasn't all. He had also been very kind.

Wally was so glad he'd come. When he grew up, he wanted to be just like his grandad.

That night, he slept surrounded by the big old whales and dreamed of his grandfather.

The Whale Point Olympics

At last, the big day arrived. The event everyone had been waiting for—the Whale Point Olympics.

It was a beautiful, sunny day, with not a cloud in the sky. Everything was perfect!

The penguins' special banner on display? Check.

Giraffe in the VIP seat? Check.

Gold, silver and bronze medals good to go? Check.

A crowd—and a big one? Check, and check!

Professor Penguin, who used to be Professor Whale's student, was master of ceremonies.

"I hereby declare the Whale Point Olympics open!" he announced. "First, Professor Whale, chair-whale of the planning committee, will say a few words."

"Ahem," said Professor Whale. "Hello, everyone. Today the sky is bluer than ever. The sea is blue, too. This makes me very happy. And I'm very happy that we can hold the Whale Point Olympics again. I will be even happier if it's a very happy day for all of you, too. In fact, I'm sure it will be. Thank you."

Everyone clapped.

"Next," Professor Penguin said, "our special guest, Giraffe, will say a few words."

When Giraffe stood up, everyone gasped to see how tall he was.

"Hello, everyone. I am Giraffe. I live in Africa. I'm Penguin's friend. Thank you so much for inviting me today. I know I'm going to have a fantastic time. And I hope you do, too. Thank you."

The crowd gave him a big hand, and those who had never seen a giraffe before, which was most of them, roared with delight.

Next, it was time for the Olympic oath. Seal, being so earnest and hardworking, had been chosen to deliver it.

"I, Seal, on behalf of all the athletes assembled here, vow that we will play fair, cheer each other on, have lots of fun and make this a very happy day."

This was greeted with the loudest applause of all. And, with a pop of fireworks, the games began.

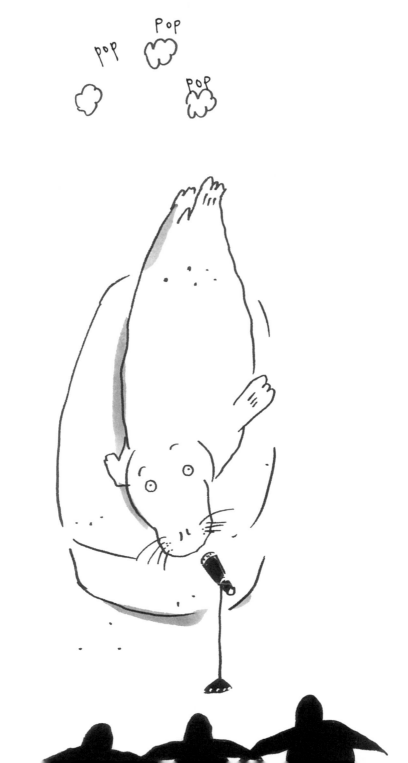

"The first event is the Seal Swimming Race,"
announced Penguin. "The starting line is
Whale Point East. Contestants must swim
around Penguin Island and back to the finish
line at Whale Point West. Seals, please go to the
starting line."

Ten seals had entered the race. Some were
confident of their speed. Others were confident
of their endurance. And some weren't
confident of either...

Professor Penguin's voice rang out. "On your
marks. Get set... Go!"

Pelican reported live from the air.

"And they're off! Look at them go!

"They're racing neck and neck. No, wait!
One of them has pulled out in front.

"It looks like...yes! It is! It's our dependable
delivery seal. What speed!

"The rest are moving in a pack."

"Seal's so fast, he's already reached Penguin Island and is circling it clockwise.

  "He's surfing the waves.

  "The other nine are almost even. Oh! One of them is falling behind. Looks like he's running out of steam.

  "He's really struggling.

  "Meanwhile, the other eight are almost at the island."

"The delivery seal has passed the halfway mark. He hasn't slowed down at all.

"Eight more are just starting around the island now.

"Oh! Here comes Seal, out the other side and heading for the finish line at Whale Point West. Look at him go!

"And the last seal is finally reaching the island."

"He looks exhausted. Hang in there! You can do it!

"Wait a minute. The delivery seal has stopped swimming. What's going on? He's heading back around the island. That's off course.

"What can he be thinking? He's gone over to the last seal. They seem to be talking.

"They've started swimming together."

"Well, I'll be. Seal's going to circle the island again.

"Oh! Here come the other eight round the island and heading straight for Whale Point! And the first one crosses the finish line! Then another and another!

"Here come the last two, quite a way behind the rest. My goodness! The delivery seal comes in last!"

Seal had kindly kept the slowest swimmer company the whole way. And that was how all ten seals made it across the finish line. Seal was beaming. He seemed very pleased with the results.

"The next event is the Penguin Walking Race," Whistler announced, taking over from Professor Penguin as master of ceremonies.

"The starting line is in front of the main stage. The finish line is at Whale Point North. Penguins, please go to the starting line."

Twenty penguins of all shapes and sizes had entered the race. Ten were from Penguin Island School.

But Professor Penguin was not one of them, having apparently decided to cheer them on instead.

"On your marks. Get set... Go!"

Pelican took up the announcing again. "What a nice, clean start.

"Flip-flap, flip-flap... Off they trot on short little legs.

"Wow! Who would've guessed they could move so fast!

"Professor Penguin's scurrying along beside them, cheering them on. He's waving a huge flag."

"It looks handmade.

"That must be the crest of Penguin Island School.

"The Professor's pretty fast. He's almost as fast as the racers.

"Oh! One of them is pulling ahead. It appears to be a student from Penguin Island School. She's picking up the pace."

"But there's no telling yet. It's too soon to call.

"Professor Penguin's still going fast.

"He's cheering and waving his flag.

"Look! The finish line is coming into sight.

"Oh no! There's a penguin down! It's the Professor!

"Professor Penguin has fallen over! He appears to have tripped on his flag."

"But what's this? Everyone's rushing towards him.

"His students are gathering around him! No, not just his students. All the other penguins, too.

"They've all stopped racing to help the Professor!

"Is he all right?

"Yes! Looks like he's okay.

"He's back on his feet."

"Are they going to restart the race?

"Oh my! Look at that. They've gone and picked up the Professor!

"And they're carrying him down the home stretch!

"As for Professor Penguin...

"...he's still waving his flag!

"And they all cross the finish line at the same time!"

A roar of applause shook Whale Point.

Pelican had been shouting so excitedly that
he was now gasping for breath.

It was clear that the students really loved
Professor Penguin.

Professor Whale's heart filled with gladness.
"He's a good teacher," he thought.

Professor Penguin returned to the podium. "And now for the climax! The Whale Spouting Contest that we've all been waiting for. Contestants, please gather at Whale Point North."

Bubbles, Whistler, Bella Balena and Professor Whale were the judges.

For the first time in many years, Whale Sea was jammed with whales. The Professor smiled.

"Now that looks more like Whale Sea, doesn't it?" Bella Balena said.

Professor Penguin faced the water. "Let the first round begin!" he shouted.

The whales had been split into five groups. They would compete to see who had the strongest, most spectacular spout, and the winner from each group would go on to the final round.

One by one, plumes of water burst into the air.

Whooosh! ... Whump!
Fwissshhhh!
Wheeeee, Kerboom!

Everyone clapped with delight.

The first round took quite a long time because there were far more whales than anyone had expected. First one group, then another, and then another competed, and one by one, the finalists were decided.

"And now for the fifth and final group!"

Young Wally was in this one.

The crowd watched closely as each spout burst into the air. The judges wrote down the scores.

Contestant 2, contestant 3, contestant 4... contestant 10. At last, it was Wally's turn.

"Here we go, Grandad," he thought, and he
spouted with all his might.

Piyooooo...splurt, splish, splash...!

Everyone cheered loudly to see the little whale
spouting as hard as he could.
And, although he didn't make it to the finals,
Wally looked very proud.

As for the five finalists, every one of them displayed the most magnificent and stupendous spouts.

"And that brings the Games to an end!" Professor Penguin announced.

The crowd burst into applause and a deafening cheer rocked Whale Point.

The Awards Ceremony

"Now for the awards ceremony," said Professor
Penguin.

Everyone turned to look at the winners'
platform.

The winners of the Swimming Race received
their medals one by one: first place, second
place, third place.

The delivery seal clapped the loudest of all.

"Next, we'll award the medals for the Walking Race," Professor Penguin said. "But first, the head judge has an announcement to make."

He looked a little sheepish. After all, it was because he had tripped that the race had not gone as planned.

"Yes, well, due to unforeseen circumstances,"
Bubbles began. "Everyone reached the finish
line at the same time, so the judges have
decided that all the contestants will win a gold
medal. However, the medals will be quite a bit
smaller."

"Yay!" the penguins shouted, hopping up and
down. "Hip-hip-hooray!"

"And last but not least," said Professor Penguin, "we will now announce the winners of the Spouting Contest. Head Judge Bubbles, please."

Everyone held their breath.

"And the winners are...for the bronze, Whalester. For the silver, Wallity. And, for the gold, Whalena!"

A great cheer rose from the crowd.

When she received her gold medal, Whalena blew one last magnificent spout. A rainbow shimmered in the spray.

"It's time for some closing remarks," said Professor Penguin. "Professor Whale?"

Once again, the Professor felt his heart filled to bursting.

What a joy it had been to meet everyone. How wonderful it had been to put on the Olympics again. And the games had been so special.

"My dear friends. Has this been a happy day for you all?

"It certainly has for me! An extraordinarily happy day.

"I'm so glad we brought back the Whale Point Olympics.

"Thank you.

"And now, I declare the Whale Point Olympics officially over."

His speech was greeted with thunderous applause.

He was so happy he could hardly bear it.

Down his cheek rolled a single (but truly humungous) teardrop, as blue as the sea and the sky.

Can I Stay?

Even after everything had been cleared away and all the others had gone home, young Wally and Professor Whale's old friends lingered on at Whale Point.

"Your spout was pretty impressive, little one," Whistler said.

His sister Bubbles nodded. "I bet you'll win the gold medal some day," she said.

"It was so pretty," Bella Balena agreed.

"It reminded me of Spout's spout," said Professor Whale. "I can tell you're his grandson."

How he wished his old friend could have been there.

For a while, they all gazed at the sunset, lost in thought.

"It's hard to say goodbye, isn't it?" said Bubbles.

"You're not kidding," Whistler agreed.

"Well then, why don't you all stay?" Professor Whale suggested.

"I wish I could," said Whistler. "But I'm about to become a grandfather."

"I'm already a grandmother and a great-grandmother, what's more—and my little ones all need me back home to teach them to spout," Bubbles said.

Professor Whale looked sad.

Just then, Wally piped up. "Uhm, may I stay?" he said. "I'd love you to teach me how to spout."

The Professor looked at him in surprise.
"But that won't do. Your parents will miss you,"
he said.

"Well, actually, I don't have any. That's why
my grandad raised me. But he's gone now...so
I'm all on my own."

The old whales fell silent, their eyes fixed on
little Wally.

"Why not, then?" Bella Balena said suddenly.
"And maybe I'll stay, too."

"But you must have children and grand-
children yourself," said Professor Whale.

"Oh. Didn't I tell you? I live on my own."

What Happened Next

What happened next, you ask?

Now, every day at Whale Point, little Wally can be seen perfecting his spout.

Piyooooo...splurt, splish, splash...
Piyooooo...splurt, splish, splash...

His personal trainer is Professor Whale, of course.

And at his side—you guessed it, Bella Balena.

The other day, Wally wrote a letter to his friend
back on Otto Island.

Dear Otty who lives at Otto Island,

How are you? I'm fine. I'm staying at Whale Point where my grandad was from. Every day, I work on spouting because when I grow up, I want to win a gold medal. So I won't be back for a while, but please don't forget me.

I'll write again soon.
Your friend,
Wally at Whale Point

He asked the delivery seal to deliver it right
away.

Which reminds me. There's a new delivery seal.
His name is Sport and he's still learning the
ropes.

Who's that, you say?

Do you remember, at the Whale Point Olympics, the slowest seal in the Swimming Race, the one Seal helped get to the finish line? That's Sport. He's been a huge fan of Seal's ever since, and says he can't wait to grow up to be just like him!

This edition first published in 2018 by Gecko Press
PO Box 9335, Wellington 6141, New Zealand
info@geckopress.com

English-language edition © Gecko Press Ltd 2018
Translation © Cathy Hirano 2018

Watashi wa Kujira-Misaki ni Sumu Kujira to Îmasu
Text copyright © 2003 by Megumi Iwasa
Illustrations copyright © 2003 by Jun Takabatake
First published in Japan in 2003 by KAISEI-SHA Publishing Co., Ltd., Tokyo
English-language translation rights arranged with KAISEI-SHA Publishing Co.,
Ltd. through Japan Foreign-Rights Centre

Distributed in the United States and Canada by Lerner Publishing Group,
lernerbooks.com
Distributed in the United Kingdom by Bounce Sales and Marketing,
bouncemarketing.co.uk
Distributed in Australia by Scholastic Australia, scholastic.com.au
Distributed in New Zealand by Upstart Distribution, upstartpress.co.nz

Edited by Jolisa Gracewood
Design and typesetting by Katrina Duncan
Printed in China by Everbest Printing Co. Ltd,
an accredited ISO 14001 & FSC certified printer

Hardback (USA) ISBN: 978-1-776572-06-9
Paperback ISBN: 978-1-776572-07-6
Ebook available

For more curiously good books, visit geckopress.com